PatCh

David Slonim

PatCh

Roaring Brook Press New York

Rabbits

Patch is my dog.
It's my job to take care of him.

Sometimes it's easy.

Sometimes it's not.

Patch likes to go for walks.

"Remember, Patch," I say,
"don't chase rabbits."

But it's hard for Patch to not chase rabbits.

He always ends up in the prickly bush.

"It's okay, Patch," I tell him.

"Tomorrow we'll try again."

Fleas

Once, Patch got fleas.

We tried flea collars.

We tried flea powder.

We even tried a special flea bath.
But nothing worked.

So he had to sleep outside.

Poor Patch.

"What are a few fleas between friends?" I said.

The Contest

One day we heard about a big contest.

So Patch and I decided to train.
"Sit!" I said. Patch sat.

"Roll over!"

"Catch!"

"Dance!"

Patch was amazing.

When the big day came, we were ready!

The other dogs went first.

They sat

and fetched

and played dead.

Then it was Patch's turn.

"Sit!" I said. Patch froze.

"Roll over!" I said. Patch didn't budge.

"Beg? Dance? Play Dead?"

Patch just stood there trembling.

Later we played in the yard, just for fun.
Patch looked like a champion.

"We're buddies through thick and thin," I said.

"No matter what."

To Bonnie

Special thanks to Chuck Neustifter

In memory of Patches

Library of Congress Cataloging-in-Publication Data

Slonim, David.
    Patch / David Slonim. — 1st ed.
        p.   cm.
    Summary: A boy shares three simple stories about his dog, Patch.
    Contents: Rabbits — Fleas — The contest.
    ISBN 978-1-59643-643-5 (hardcover)
[1. Dogs—Fiction.]   I. Title.
    PZ7.S6338Pat 2013
    [E]—dc23
                                                    2012029545

Roaring Brook Press books are available for special promotions and premiums.
For details contact: Director of Special Markets, Holtzbrinck Publishers.

First edition 2013
Book design by Andrew Arnold
Printed in China by Macmillan Production (Asia) Ltd.,
Kowloon Bay, Hong Kong (Supplier 10)

1 3 5 7 9 10 8 6 4 2